Vulcan:
An Alien Scifi Romance

DEMELZA CARLTON

ONE

"Romance again? You can't be serious. Didn't we do that theme last month?" Sunita exclaimed.

Hestia shook her head. "Last month it was mysteries, then science, before this month's inspirational books. The month before that it was historical romance. Tomorrow we start romantic suspense.

Totally different."

"They're both still romance subgenres," Reina chimed in. "Stars, there are enough of them to just run romance every month, and readers will borrow them. Everyone wants a little more love in their life, even if it's only the fictional kind."

"The fictional kind are always better than real life. They don't leave hair in the shower," Sunita said.

"So why are you complaining about having romance again?" Reina asked.

Sunita shrugged. "Because every time we have a romance theme, I have to deal with a bunch of cranky men readers who only want manly books, not girls' stuff."

"I can't believe misogyny still exists. Shouldn't we have bred it out of the

Human race by now? Or the Titan one?" Reina complained.

"Misogyny isn't genetic, it's about environmental and emotional factors, particularly in childhood. Stamping out an idea isn't as simple as a genetic patch. Especially one as seductive as the thought that you're better than someone else, or a whole group of people," Hestia said.

"Like how people who read are more intelligent and interesting than people who don't?" Reina asked.

"Obviously," Sunita said.

Hestia couldn't argue with that. She was the Colony's only qualified librarian, after all. Reina and Sunita were both fast learners and extremely helpful in keeping the library running. Especially when New

Hope was about to complete another orbit around its star, Altan, and they changed themes. A new year called for a new book, or at least that's what the sign over the themed display said.

It was more than just a new book for the three of them, though. On the last day of New Hope's year, they checked which books had been borrowed in the last month, put them onto the regular shelves, then took the unwanted ones downstairs for storage. At the same time, the printing presses got to work on the next set of themed books, printing brand new paperback copies from the electronic books in the archives, to fill those themed shelves for the next nineteen-day orbital period.

New Year's Eve was important. Out

with the old, in with the new, and when they'd finished work for the day…

"Are you going there again tonight?" Sunita asked.

Hestia kept her eyes on the shelves she was stacking. "Going where?"

"You know."

Hestia sighed. "And what if I am?"

Sunita cocked her head to the side. "If I'd known, the first night I got invitations for the three of us and dragged you along, that you'd end up spending every New Year's Eve at Forge, drooling over the dancers like one of those misogynists at a peep show, I never would have taken you. It's not healthy, Hestia."

"That's not what you said before. That first time, you said it wasn't healthy for me to go home every night, and I needed to get out more. Now going out isn't healthy, either?" Hestia snapped. "And I don't drool. The dancers in Forge aren't strippers, either. They're performers, artists, and they do it with their clothes on. There's a reason tickets to Forge sell out every New Year's Eve. Everyone there wants to party, sending off the old year and ringing in the new, hoping for a fresh start."

"But not you," Reina said softly. "What's your new year's resolution this year?"

Hestia folded her arms across her chest. "The same as the last time I told you. To survive the year. I owe it to Ayumu."

The memory of the last time she'd

seen Ayumu, raising their glasses together in a toast to a different new year, on a different planet, flashed through her mind for only a moment, but it was long enough to bring tears to her eyes. If only he were here. She had so much she wanted to say to him.

"You owe it to Ayumu's memory to live, not just survive," Sunita scolded. "What you should do is make that your resolution tonight. To actually live. And then do it, if only for the next nineteen days. I guarantee you won't be drooling over dancers next New Year's Eve if you do."

She didn't drool. "I won't – " Hestia began hotly.

"Just try it," Reina coaxed. "It's less than three weeks. Most resolutions don't last that long, even with a normal Earth year. I'll tell you what. If you change your New Year's resolution tonight, we'll let you pick the next theme and we won't argue at all. You can have a whole year of poetry, even if you're the only one who'll read any of it."

"Not true. One of the library patrons keeps requesting a poetry theme every month. Seeing as we're doubling up on romance, to cater for the majority, it makes sense to give people what they should read, instead of just what they want every month. I bet we have a lot of people borrowing poetry books if we had that as a theme!"

Both women folded their arms.

"Make a new resolution, and we'll see," Sunita said.

Hestia knew when she was beaten. "We'll see," she echoed.

A new resolution wasn't so hard. It wasn't like she had to keep it. If they'd asked her to stay away from Forge, she wouldn't have agreed, but this…maybe. Maybe…

In the darkness of Forge, after the dancers left the stage, with a drink in her hand as they counted down the seconds, then she could make her decision. And not before.

TWO

Vulcan set the video to replay from the beginning. Something just wasn't right. Sure, it was a whirl of light and colour, the beat like a heart drumming the countdown to year's end, but he looked stiff, stilted, instead of the delicate flow of movement Wakana had always been able to demonstrate on this traditional

New Year dance.

"Good news, boss. Nang Tani called and said the banana order should be here within the hour. Daquiris are back on the menu, thank the stars."

Vulcan didn't take his eyes off the video. "Thanks, Nihal. Can you take a look at this? It's missing something, and I can't work out what."

Nihal oozed around the desk — she was full-blooded djinn, so she could do that — and peered at the screen. After a long moment, she said, "Well, it's flat, boss, that's what it is. If you want people to fall asleep during the performance, it's fine, but if you want them to celebrate the New Year…you need fireworks."

Vulcan stared at the screen, then flicked his fingers. On the video, a light show erupted around the dancers, one that hadn't been there last time he watched the video. It still wasn't enough, though…

"You ever get tired of celebrating the New Year?" he asked. This would be his nineteenth New Year's Eve party in the Colony – one for every Academy dancer who'd died. He'd left Wakana 'til last because he knew he couldn't do her favourite dance justice. He looked…dead.

Nihal grinned. "Yep. About an hour or two after midnight, every time. When the show's over, right after I call for last drinks, everyone starts heading home, and I can see the end of my shift. Until then, I'll be the life of the party, keeping the drinks flowing, while you deliver another performance that'd make your Academy proud."

The Alba Academy of Dance was no more. He was the last one left. Yet energy and art never died, it stayed in the universe to inspire new forms in the future. At least, that's what Wakana had believed. And it was in her memory that he danced tonight. If she were here, she'd be rolling around on the floor, laughing her many tails off, at his piss-poor performance. He was a shambling zombie to her light-footed quest for perfection. Better to be a joker, a trickster, for Wakana said illusion and trickery lay at the heart of this dance.

Tonight would be the last performance, he promised himself. A swan song, though he wouldn't be singing. He'd send Wakana out with the bang she deserved. If Nihal wanted fireworks, that's what she'd get. By the end of the night, nobody would be able to see, the celebration would blaze so bright.

And when the New Year began, it truly would be a fresh start.

THREE

When the bouncer waved her in to Forge, Hestia smoothed her dress self-consciously before stepping inside. This was the only occasion when she ever wore a dress, and this was the only dress she owned, bought for that first New Year's Eve party at Sunita's insistence. Even in the beginning, Forge had enforced a strict dress code. Then, she thought the dress a ridiculous extravagance that she'd never wear again.

Now…it was a costume that let her remember what it had been like to have hopes and dreams and family. If only for a night.

From the queue outside, she'd have expected the place to be packed, but she'd also have been wrong. Forge wasn't the sort of place that packed people in like sardines. Every patron had space, a seat, and no trouble ordering as many drinks as they desired. Or as many as they could afford, which was far more than Hestia's meagre librarian salary allowed for, judging by the number of patrons who passed out at every party. It was an exclusive bar, and its New Year's

Eve celebration even more exclusive still. She still couldn't believe that they accepted her application for an invitation every time. Yet here she was, breezing between the tables to the bar, her skirt swishing around her with every step.

The bartender greeted her with a wide white smile and, "The usual?"

Hestia nodded.

The bartender leaned forward. "Might I suggest switching the strawberry daquiri for a banana one? We've had to use flavour syrups for all of them until now, but tonight we have real bananas."

Hestia's mouth watered. She hadn't eaten a banana since she left Earth. Maybe having a different drink would be enough change to satisfy Sunita. Even Sunita couldn't deny the difference between flavour syrup and real fruit was not dissimilar to the chasm between surviving and actually living.

"All right," Hestia said, holding out her credit chip so the bartender could scan her payment.

The payment processed, as Hestia knew it would, and the girl behind the bar promised to bring them out to her when they were ready.

"Only the daquiri now. The other one later," Hestia said, imagining both drinks arriving together just as the show started, when she'd have no choice but to drink the second one warm instead of chilled when she'd finished the first.

The bartender nodded. "Of course. Not until the show is over."

It was Hestia's turn to nod, letting the

relief relax her. All her life, people had ignored her, getting things wrong and insisting it was her fault, so she'd given up complaining, but the staff in Forge treated her differently. That's why she kept coming back. For one night, they made her feel like she mattered, instead of being a nobody who hid in the library and read books the rest of the time.

As she slid into her seat at the table on the balcony closest to the stage, she finally allowed herself to relax completely. She'd made it on time — early, as the show hadn't started yet — but close enough to starting time that they'd already turned the lights down. A pity, because if there'd been light enough to read, she would have pulled out her book. Oh, she had access to every book in the database from her tablet, but it just wasn't the same as turning real pages.

"Your drink, ma'am." Someone set the cocktail on the table, then left.

Hestia wrinkled her nose. Really, they thought she was old enough to be a ma'am and not a miss?

She pulled the oversized glass toward her and sucked at the straw. She nearly moaned as the sweet, frozen nectar hit her tongue. Best…daquiri…ever. The servers could call her whatever they liked as long as they served this sort of ambrosia. She wished she'd ordered two.

Hestia half rose from her seat, ready to go back to the bar to do just that.

A deep, steady beat rose from the floor, vibrating through her feet as it filled the bar with the thumping sound, silencing all conversation.

Hestia found herself perched eagerly on the edge of her seat again, awaiting the show. The drumming heartbeat quickened, until it beat as fast as her own thrumming heart.

That's when he appeared, in the centre of the stage. Vulcan, the star of the show. Then the drum beat once more and he dropped, spreadeagled on the stage.

Hestia fancied her heart stopped at the sight.

Then, slowly, the beat started up again, more performers appearing in a circle around him, almost by magic, until there were twenty of them on the stage. No, nineteen. No…Hestia tried to count, but then the dancers began to move, and she had to give up as they spun and whirled, merging and parting, never still…

Until he moved. Like a corpse arising from the grave, stiff and jerky, until he stood tall above the other dancers, who rushed at him. One moment they were all in a huddle in the middle of the stage, and then they vanished, so he stood there alone in the spotlight.

Not that Hestia would have noticed anyone else.

The music shifted, and so did he, becoming the swift creature that sniffed at the crowd, hunting for something, before he whirled like the other dancers had, revealing his tail…no, tails, Hestia thought, as the man flew about the stage as if gravity could not hold him.

Her breath caught in her throat. From

corpse to fox to swirling stardust, he became her entire galaxy, pulling her very soul into the singularity at her core.

FOUR

When he'd first started to dance on stage, Vulcan had been told to ignore the crowd. He danced for an audience of one. When he stepped out onto the stage, he only needed to lock eyes with one person, and that was who he danced for, until the song ended. Never mind if it was a stranger or the one he loved most — no one else mattered, except his one connection in the room.

He'd since learned that it was better to make several connections over the course of his set, for the more people he charmed with his performance, the longer they stayed, and the more money they parted with.

Tonight, he danced for Wakana, whose spirit he hoped would be somewhere in the audience, but he knew he danced for the living, too. So after he'd crawled out of his illusory grave, he looked up.

And there she was, like every other New Year's Eve, perched on the edge of her balcony seat, gripping the railing like she was ready to jump down and join him.

Yet something in her gaze buzzed with life, humming through his body like he'd touched an electrical main. Vulcan grinned, and sent his power out right to the edges of the stage, where the nineteen shadows of Academy dancers burst into illusory life for one last show. Music ran through his veins instead of blood, and it was like the exhilaration of applause on opening night when the full cast took to the stage.

Until the music approached its final bars, and Vulcan knew their time was done. Yet he was the one to vanish, yielding the stage to the shades of the dead, brilliantly lit and dancing as they had in life, until they took their final bow to tumultuous applause.

One blink and the stage was empty,

amid gasps from the audience. Then the lights glowed into life again, dispelling the illusion, as the servers marched out among the patrons to take drink orders. Nihal, the general of this small army, stood at the bar, pouring champagne. Or perhaps it was Colony-created sparkling fizz – it was hard to tell the difference without tasting it. Not that he'd touch the fizz – tonight called for real champagne, to drink to the end of the Academy, and whatever new start he decided on for tomorrow.

Vulcan showered quickly, dressed in his bar blacks, then headed for Nihal.

She had his drink ready, as always – an icy jug of water he wanted to down in one gulp, though it usually took several – but his gaze lingered on the fizz. "Do we have any of the champagne on ice tonight?" he asked.

A sharp nod. "More than usual. None of the high rollers have ordered any yet. We're doing a good trade in daquiris, though — we may run out of bananas tonight."

He nodded. "I'll order more in the morning." Or the afternoon. Whenever he got into the office tomorrow. Tonight, he wanted to stay a while. The end of mourning meant living again, and toasting the New Year properly. He jerked his head toward the stage. "What's the single girl on the balcony drinking?"

Nihal's eyebrows rose. "You're in luck. I was just about to send someone over with her glass of fizz."

Perfect. "Don't bother." He busied

himself behind the bar, setting out an ice bucket and two glasses, before digging out a bottle of champagne. They'd been stored in stasis on the *Genesis*, in the luggage of some rich bastard who'd never made it onto the ship. He'd had to pull quite a few favours from Humans and Titans to secure them for his cellar, but it had been worth it. Sure, it had made his bar the neutral territory where organised crime bosses could meet with their rivals, which wasn't without risk, but crime bosses had money to burn, and fifty-year-old Earth delicacies definitely made an impression.

Nihal just watched him. "Is she someone special, boss?"

Tonight, she'd been his muse, with one look, breathing life where there had been only death…you couldn't put a price on the gift she'd given him tonight. Wine paled in comparison. It was the least he could do. "Yes," he said, lifting the tray high like he'd been taught back on Alba. Before the Academy. But not before he'd learned to move with the music.

FIVE

"You ordered a drink, ma'am?"

Twice in one night? Before she could think, Hestia grumbled, "I'm a miss, not a ma'am." Then she clapped a hand over her mouth. She never complained — no good ever came of it. She waited for the server's slick apology. It was only a matter of time before she'd find herself apologising for her outburst, far more profusely than he would.

Except…it never came.

"Then you won't object if I sit here, miss," the server said, setting his tray on the table before sliding into the seat across from her.

Dressed in black with a smile that would charm the pants off anyone, male or female, she had to admit he was sexier than most of the other servers she'd seen. Then she saw what was on his tray.

"You've got the wrong person. I ordered a glass of fizz, not…a whole bottle of Earth wine that costs more than I earn in a year. An Earth year, not an Altan one." She met his eyes. "You must be new." She'd certainly never seen him before — she'd remember if she had.

Stars, she'd have dreamed about him if she had.

"Not new. Just…giving Nihal a hand. New Year's our busiest night." The sexy server nodded at the bartender who'd taken Hestia's order. Nihal nodded back.

Hestia wet her lips. If this were a romance novel, this would be her lucky night. Mr Sexy here would whisk her away to a night of debauchery that would end in true love and a happy ever after. If it was a thriller, or some sort of mystery, whoever found her dead body tomorrow morning would uncover a trail of clues leading back to a conspiracy bigger than they'd ever imagined.

She shook her head. This was real life, not a book, and Mr Sexy deserved to know he was wasting his time. Especially as he was already reaching for the wine bottle.

"I'm a widow," she blurted out. "My fiancé was a stasis technician, building stasis pods for the *Genesis* at the Exodus spacedock. One of the perks of working at Exodus was that they allowed family to live with the staff. Instead of paying college accommodation fees on Earth, I could stay in his apartment at Exodus and get free room and board while I did my studies remotely. We were saving all our money for a wedding back home on Earth when the *Genesis* was finished. We were only weeks away from being sent home, when we went to a New Year's Eve party at one of the bars on Exodus. A few drinks, dancing to the live band, ringing in the New Year with a few more drinks, before stumbling home to sleep it off until we woke up sometime in the afternoon on New Year's Day with little more than a hangover."

She pressed her lips together grimly, then went on before Mr Sexy could interrupt. "I woke up here in the Colony. Sixty years later, fifty light years from home, in a hospital on a planet I'd never heard of. While I'd been asleep, terrorists attacked the space elevator between Exodus and Earth, and when the space elevator ripped free of the station, a fire started in the corridor where we had our apartment. Now, Ayumu, my fiancé, knowing how much I hated the risk of being in space, had scrounged up some spare parts from the workshop, and turned our bunks into emergency stasis chambers. The fire alarm activated mine, putting me into stasis without even waking me. Ayumu…he didn't make it, the nurse told me when they revived me. They'd had so little time between the attack and leaving on the *Genesis*, that they'd decided to keep me in stasis, instead of reviving me and putting me under again. They didn't even revive me until after the war, because they didn't have a suitable hospital to assess my condition until the Colony was opened. The first I knew about the war was what they told me, and if I hadn't seen so many of them, I'd find it hard to believe Titans exist. So if you're looking for a suitable one-night stand to top off your New Year, look somewhere else. I'm a widow in mourning who never even got her wedding, halfway across the galaxy from a home and a husband I'll never see again." Tears blurred her vision, but she forced herself to finish. "There's your backstory infodump, in all its amateur tackiness. If you're sensible, you'll send me back to the slush pile where I belong, and go find some breakout bestseller to bed instead. So take that bottle back to the bar, before you get into trouble for it, and send someone over with my glass of fizz. Now I've remembered what brought me here, I want nothing more than to forget, and that's what the fizz is for."

Warm fingers curled around hers, pressing the stem of a glass into her hand. She heard the pop of the bottle, before something glugged into the glass she now held.

"In vino veritas, or in wine there is truth. Far better than that artificial fizz, I promise you. This is my bottle, and I can think of no one better to share it with than you, especially now I know your backstory, as you put it. We shall drink to the departed together, for I'm here to mourn, too. And, lovely lady who has lost everything, I will tell you a secret that no one else knows, seeing as you have been so honest with me, and then you may judge who has lost more – you, or me."

Hestia blinked away her tears and looked up to meet his enquiring gaze. Yes, there was a full glass of wine in her hand, and another in his.

A sensible woman would tell him she

wasn't interested, and send him away. But Hestia was a sucker for a good story, and she hadn't had real wine since Earth.

Just one wouldn't hurt…

Live a little, a small voice in her head whispered. It almost sounded like Sunita.

SIX

He'd admitted to her he was mourning, too – how much harder would it be to tell her who? He'd nearly told Nihal a couple of times, but then she'd said something about how he did the Academy proud, and he'd closed his mouth on so many words unsaid.

She lifted the glass to her lips, her eyes

on him. Then she sipped and closed her eyes.

Seconds passed. A tear trickled down her cheek. "The last time I had real wine like this was my twenty-first birthday, back on Earth," she breathed. Then she set the glass down and shook her head. "I'm sorry, I – "

He interrupted, "Do you want to know why I do them, a different show every New Year's Eve? Dance alone, when I should be one of the crowd, let someone else be the star?" His voice had come out too harsh. Vulcan cleared his throat and continued, "Back on Alba, an inhabited moon in the Titan system, or at least it was, there was a dance company that only took the very best. In a system full of superhumans, it was an impossible dream for all but a select few. That's like…being accepted into the Bolshoi Ballet on Earth.

"And… a few short months before the robots rebelled and threw all the Titans out of the system, by some miracle or madness, they accepted me. I thought it was a joke, or a scam, when I first got the letter, but it was neither. Those months were the hardest and the happiest of my life. A dream I didn't want to wake up from. Just to breathe the same air as some of those performers..." Vulcan shook his head. He was a dancer, not a poet – he didn't have the words to describe it. "We were flown to the *Titanic* in the first wave of the evacuation, before even some of the government leaders. Something about preserving Titan art and culture, or that's what we were told. The others just accepted it, because they were the epitome of Alban arts, but me, I…" Again, he shook his head. "It was even worse when we woke up from stasis. That's when I found out they hadn't managed to evacuate everybody. That some people had been left behind, likely to die at the hands of the robots. People who might have been better at settling a brand-new star system, instead of a bunch of dancers.

"So when they called for volunteers to help explore the planets here, I signed up. Because the sooner we found a planet, the sooner there'd be an Altan Academy of Dance, or at least that's what I told the others. I just felt so useless, and I wanted to do something…"

Vulcan swallowed. This was the hardest part. "They loaded me up with enough weapons to blow up a small moon, and an armoured suit that'd make sure I survived the explosion, too. They put me on a team headed by Ghost, Nihal's brother. Achilles, Prometheus…all the others were way more experienced at working in vacuum…and sent us to Gamma. The second planet from the sun.

"The danger was supposed to be planetside – where we were exploring the unknown. The *Titanic* was simply sitting in the asteroid belt between Delta and Elysium, replenishing vital resources. Water, oxygen, fuel…using nothing more than space tugs. One of the tugs malfunctioned, so instead of slowing down as it approached the *Titanic* with its payload, it sped up and…well, if it had just holed the ship, it would've been bad, but reparable. Bulkheads sealing around the damaged sections, that sort of thing. Even with the engines hit, it would've been reparable. Only the collision with the tug sent the ship deeper into the asteroid belt and with the engines hit, there was no time. Some people made it to escape pods, but with all our exploration vessels out, the Academy dancers had taken one of the empty flight decks as a dance studio, planning a performance to celebrate our new start in a new system. The one closest to the engines, where the tug hit. All the dancers, and all the instructors were there — everyone in the Academy. No survivors."

Vulcan swallowed. Now he'd started, he had to finish the tale. "I think that's when it hit me, as hard as a space tug. That with the Academy gone, as long as we still had the people from the Academy, we'd be able to rebuild. But that day, the Academy died, and any dream I'd ever had of becoming a dancer like they were died with them. There were no bodies to bury, no funerals, nowhere we could all come together to mourn those we'd lost because the *Titanic* was gone, too, and everyone was scattered to the smaller ships, at least until the Colony opened. I couldn't start a new Academy here, even if I'd wanted to – but on a smaller stage, with maybe not as much light…I might be able to bring them to life again, if only for a night…and that's where the first New Year's Eve party at Forge came from. Each performance honouring a different dancer's life, even if I can only manage a dim shadow of their brilliance, because they're not really there…"

Vulcan flicked a finger, and twenty finger-sized figures appeared on the table, dancing just as they had on stage tonight. They spun, circled, converged…and then vanished. Never to return. Vale, Wakana, and everyone else, too.

The woman's eyes were wide as she stared from the table top to him and back again. "You're Vulcan," she breathed. "And all the other performers are…your illusions? I always thought they were real!" She set her glass down on the table. "I've never seen anyone do anything like that. What are you?"

If he hadn't already known she was Human, that would have clinched it. No Titan asked another what sort of creature they were — it was considered rude. Yet he couldn't bring himself to take offence at her wide-eyed curiosity.

"I'm an ifrit. Half djinn, half…something else corporeal. In my case, half demon." Which was why he'd been sent to explore Gamma — his heat tolerance and natural talent for manipulating electromagnetic radiation, though he was better at visible light than other frequencies. To demonstrate, he conjured a red light that lit his face from below, which made even the most beautiful face look demonic.

She didn't look repulsed, though. If anything, she leaned forward, closer. "Here I thought you were just the most incredible dancer I'd ever seen. Now you tell me you're the only dancer on the stage, and while you dance, you're controlling a couple dozen other illusion dancers, so lifelike I would never have guessed they weren't real? Your Academy was lucky to have you."

She was Human, she'd never seen Academy dancers perform, so she couldn't possibly understand how clumsy he looked compared to any of them. She wasn't even that observant. "Nineteen, not two dozen. There were twenty of us." He ticked them off on his fingers. "Nineteen New Year's Eve parties, nineteen performances, each mourning and celebrating a different dancer. This was my final show."

As if on cue, the DJ played the first strains of the traditional final song of the year.

Vulcan rose to his feet, raising his glass.

SEVEN

Auld Lang Syne began to play, and Hestia forgot all about the dancer. Should old acquaintance be forgot? she scolded herself, bringing her glass to her lips. No, she would never forget Ayumu, though he'd never take her hand again as he stood beside her, getting all the words wrong as he tried to sing the ancient song. She took a gulp, nearly choking as the rich flavour reminded her this was real wine and not fake fizz.

The song faded, and she swiped a hand across her eyes to scrub away the tears. Everyone took up the countdown,

Three!

Two!

One!

HAPPY NEW YEAR!

Vulcan inclined his head to her and touched his glass to hers.

Completely the opposite to her last new year with Ayumu, who'd wrapped his arms around her and kissed her breathless. Stars, what she'd give for someone to kiss her like that again. Ayumu never would, but maybe…

Live a little, Sunita's voice seemed to

whisper again.

Hestia drained her glass. Liquid courage, that's what she'd heard it called back on Earth. Stars, she'd never dare do this sober. She was second-guessing herself even now. If she hesitated, all was lost.

She closed the distance between her and Vulcan, threw her arms around his neck, glass and all, and kissed him.

EIGHT

A better man would have pulled away. A less broken man might have managed to resist. But no one else had been on the stage that first night, when he'd wanted to fall to his knees under the weight of his grief. When his memory had dragged him back to Prochoros's oft-repeated advice: "Dance for an audience of one."

But which one? Of all the dancers at the Academy, how could he choose only one?

He'd raised his eyes to heaven in despair, but on the way up he'd been caught in her gaze and couldn't break free.

Drawing a perfect image in his mind of another pair of mesmerising eyes — they'd belonged to Horea, an iele who could seduce with a glance. And when the man moved…the dance had been so hypnotic, even Vulcan had forgotten himself.

She was his audience, and for her, Vulcan had become Horea's reflection from the other side of the void.

Nineteen nights she had been his muse, his inspiration, and if her price was a kiss, then he would give it gladly. Before stealing a kiss for himself, from inspiration personified.

She began it, and she had to end it, for Vulcan was at her command, whether she knew it or not.

Yet when she broke the kiss, pulling back, his heart broke a little, too.

"Happy New Year," she said breathlessly, then turned to go.

"Wait!" he said, grabbing her hand.

She turned and stared. First at his hand, before her wide eyes rose to meet his.

He should let go. But he couldn't seem to force his fingers to open.

She could tug her hand free. She should, because he couldn't.

Yet there they stood, an island of

stillness in the midst of the movement that was a New Year's Eve celebration at Forge.

"Stay," he said, at the same time as she said, "I should go."

Vulcan swallowed. "Take the rest of the wine, then." He thrust the ice bucket at her.

He could see the refusal in her eyes.

"I'll walk you home, and carry it for you," he said.

She shook her head. "I don't need any more to drink. I think I've had enough for tonight."

"Tell me your New Year's resolution, then," he suggested, setting the bucket back on the table.

She blew out a breath. "Why does anyone care so much about those things?"

"I'll tell you mine, if you tell me yours," Vulcan said.

She raised her eyebrows, as if daring him to go first.

He took a deep breath. "I'm going to stop mourning. The Academy and everyone in it is gone, taking my dreams with it. This was my last performance. It's time to move on and try something new."

She seized his hand in both of hers. "You can't! New Year won't be the if you don't take the stage at Forge! It's the only time I can forget…"

They both needed to forget. "There are better ways to escape life than drinking in dark bars," Vulcan said. "I'll show you tomorrow, if you let me. Only permit me to see you home safely tonight, so I'll know where to pick you up tomorrow."

NINE

For as long as she could remember, she'd had it drummed into her never to let a man know where she lived unless she trusted him. She barely knew Vulcan, yet she was ready to let him walk her home. If this were a romance novel, she'd invite him in when she got there, and then…

Hestia shook herself. She wasn't a

romance heroine. Not now, not ever. Heroines didn't lose the man they loved. They got to live happily ever after.

The sensible side of her said to call for a skimmer, like she usually did.

But she still held Vulcan's hand, and the reassuring strength of it was doing strange things to her insides. She wanted to know what else he could do with his hands.

That wasn't just living a little. That was taking life by the asteroids and…

"Yes," she breathed.

Hand in hand, they went to the bar, where Vulcan handed the ice bucket to the bartender. She fitted a seal over the top of the bottle, presumably so he could enjoy the rest of the priceless bottle later.

"I'm going to see Miss…er…"

Hestia almost laughed. She hadn't even told him her name! But the bartender knew, for she'd surely seen it when she'd scanned her ID chip. She didn't seem inclined to help him out, though.

"I'm Hestia," she said.

"I'm going to see Miss Hestia home safely," Vulcan announced.

"Sure, boss," the bartender said, then turned to Hestia. "Want me to call a skimmer?"

She didn't really need a skimmer. It was only a short walk across the city to her home. Hestia still wasn't sure why she'd picked an apartment in Metropolis City instead of one of the satellite domes, except that it had been close to the hospital and the library, the only two places she'd ventured out to in those first few frightening days. Now, her apartment had begun to feel like home, so she hadn't seriously considered moving.

That it was walking distance to Forge might have been a consideration, too…

Not that she'd ever fantasised about walking home with Vulcan before.

Well, not for more than a moment or two. Her thoughts had been more about what they'd do when they reached her house…

Hestia felt her cheeks redden. Not for the first time, she was glad of the dim lighting in the club.

A romantic night-time walk with Vulcan would be lovely.

Then again, there had been that

murder not long ago…and sometimes fights broke out in the streets between Humans and Titans who didn't want the war to be over. A skimmer was safer. And they'd be at her house faster, in case he wanted to…

"Yes, please," Hestia said. She was mad to even think it, but that didn't matter.

All too soon, they stood out the front of Forge as the skimmer glided to the ground in front of them. Vulcan offered her a hand to help her up onto the narrow platform, like some aristocrat in a historical romance. Hestia was no shy debutante – she didn't hesitate.

She'd barely settled herself on the skimmer when she felt the heat of him close behind her. Then her breath caught in her throat as he pressed against her, all hard muscle, especially that bulge pressing against her lower back. Was he really that big?

"I thought these things were big enough for two. Two of you, maybe," Vulcan grumbled in her ear.

Stars help her, but she could feel his voice rumbling through her chest, and it did things to her heart, and other parts besides. Maybe she would emulate a historical romance heroine and swoon. Then he'd have to carry her inside to bed and…

"Destination?" the skimmer asked.

"Home, please," Hestia said breathlessly, holding her hand over the scanner so it could get the address off her chip. She wasn't sure she could manage to get the words out without her brain going somewhere else entirely.

One thing was certain. When they arrived, she definitely wanted to invite him inside. None of that kissing goodbye on the doorstep stuff. If she was going to live instead of just survive this year, she was starting right now.

TEN

When the skimmer glided to the ground in front of Hestia's home, Vulcan couldn't help but laugh. "I knew I'd seen you before – and I'll bet you know far more about safe ways to escape than I ever will. You're the Colony librarian!"

She stiffened against him. "What's wrong with that?"

He didn't want to move away from her, but they had to get off the skimmer. He forced himself to step down and hold out a hand to help her. "It means my plan to introduce you to the joys of reading the library collection just fizzled like a wet firework. You should be the one instructing me. I bow to your superior expertise." And he did, just to see the surprise on her face.

She took his hand and leaped lightly to the pavement. "You're nothing like I expected."

"How did you imagine I'd be?" he asked.

Even in the light from the streetlights, he clearly saw her blush. Her mouth opened, but no words came out. All she could do was shake her head as her blush deepened.

Ah, that quaint Earth modesty. He'd heard about it, but this was the first time he'd seen it. It only made him like her more. She was unique, his muse.

"I won't pry," he said softly, then pulled the champagne bottle out of his coat pocket. It had been squashed awkwardly between them for the skimmer ride, pressing uncomfortably into his guts as well as her back, but he'd been determined to bring it along. He held it out to her now, a peace offering. "Here. To drink while you're reading tonight."

She wrapped her fingers around the bottle, then had to grab it with both hands. "This was what was bulging at my back all the way here?" There was that blush again.

Wait, she'd thought it was him? Vulcan couldn't help but laugh. "Of course! Stars, what sort of man do you think I am?" He shook his head. "Happy New Year, Hestia. I hope it's a better one than the ones that came before." He turned to walk back to Forge.

"Wait! Do you want to come up for a drink – help me finish the bottle?"

Yes, if that's what she wanted. Anything she asked of him, he'd give it to her. "I'd be delighted, but I'll tell you now, if I do come inside, I'll have an ulterior motive."

She just stared at him, her luminous eyes beaming through the dark just like they had that first impossible night.

"Will you tell me what this year's

theme is in the library? You keep it so hush-hush, until the big reveal, and I've been waiting to see my preference hit the shelves."

She blinked, then said, "Romantic suspense."

"Ah." Vulcan's shoulders slumped. Maybe next time. He'd waited this long. "Well, now I can't refuse. Lead the way, lovely lady."

She gave him one last inscrutable look before she palmed the door open and waved him inside.

ELEVEN

Hestia led him through the library, letting the motion sensors flick the overhead lamps on to light her way.

"Ah, so that's what romantic suspense looks like," Vulcan said.

She turned to see he'd stopped in front of the display.

"Oh, look, that's me!"

Now she had to look. Stars, it did look like him. "You were a model, too?"

He laughed. "I had a friend who was trying to start up a photography business. I helped her out, posed for some portfolio shots. I never thought she'd turn me into *The Alban Assassin*, though. Ha, I wasn't holding a knife in the original shot, though – I think it was a hairbrush."

Hestia swallowed. "I can put it on reserve for you, if you like. So you can see how realistic the author's portrayal of you is, or isn't."

He raised his hands in surrender. "Oh, I'm no assassin. I'll let someone else enjoy reading that. Hopefully someone who doesn't know me. Now, when you feature the books I'm really interested in, then I might ask for a special reserve."

Now was her chance, for she doubted she'd get an opening like that again.. "What are you interested in, Vulcan?"

For a moment, his eyes seemed to smoulder, and her breath caught in her throat.

Then he ducked his head, and the moment was gone. "You're going to laugh."

"Librarian rule one: never laugh at anyone's passion for reading, no matter what the subject."

He raised an eyebrow. "That's rule one?"

He had her there. "It's my rule one. I think the one in the textbook is about making sure books are returned, and levying appropriate punishments like suspending memberships if they aren't. Providing information without judgement is still high on the official list, though. Book censorship is bad."

He took a deep breath. "Poetry, which lifts the veil from the hidden beauty of the world. The true origins of romance, from pre-literate times on Earth."

Hestia felt laughter bubbling up in her throat and tried to smother it, but failed. "You! You're the one who keeps voting for poetry."

Vulcan bowed. "I told you you'd laugh. And yes, that is me."

Hestia closed her eyes. Sunita and Reina had promised, hadn't they? If she changed her resolution, they'd let her have poetry. Let her and Vulcan have poetry. If she dared…

But that was weeks away. Right now, she felt the strangest urge to share something she'd never dared show anyone. She reached for Vulcan's arm, feeling the hard muscle that he'd gained through years of training, dancing. "Can you keep a secret?" she asked.

He grinned. "Absolutely."

"Then I want to show you something else before we go upstairs," she said, pressing her palm to the elevator controls.

TWELVE

"Welcome to the Crypt," she said, as she stepped out of the elevator. Glass panels lined the walls of the large room, and behind them…

"Are those real wood?" Vulcan exclaimed, peering at the nearest one.

Hestia nodded. "Some super rich Earth man who'd bought a place on the

Genesis to come to the Colony had his entire collection of rare books and their bookcases in stasis in the hold. He was killed in the terrorist attack on the space elevator, but all his books were already aboard. The stasis containers were cracked open the same week they woke me, and as the only qualified librarian in the system, I got offered the job of taking care of them. I agreed, but only if I could have a public library with books anyone could borrow, too. I get a monthly paper allocation for print books, most of which goes into the theme books, but if there's any left, I print copies of these from the scans on the database. There are first editions of Shakespeare's folios..."

Vulcan found himself nodding. "If

music be the food of love, play on."

Hestia's smile was sad. "The appetite may sicken, and so die." She took a deep breath. "When I woke up alone, and heard my fiancé was dead, I considered…I thought about…but someone had to preserve these books. Those first few weeks, I spent as much time as I could in here. Reina and Sunita, my assistants, called it the Crypt, where books go to die. But books never die, even if their authors do. They took me to your first show. It was my first time out in the Colony, in public, since they woke me up. I felt so lost, and then I saw you, and there was something about the way you danced…"

Vulcan nodded. He'd been just as lost, but he'd found his courage in her eyes.

He enfolded her hands in his. "The universe would be a darker place without you in it. If you ever feel that sort of despair again, please, come to me first, so I can convince you to stay."

Her eyes were wide, but she ducked her head before she disengaged her hands from his. "It happens less and less now. It's just…Ayumu. There's so many things I wanted to tell him. I never even got to say goodbye."

Vulcan swallowed. He couldn't bring the man back, but he could do something. "If you want, I could create an illusion of him, so you can say what you need to. It won't be him, and it won't be able to talk back to you, but it'll look like him, if you have a picture or maybe a video…"

She had her tablet in her hands, swiping her finger feverishly across the screen before she held it up. "Here."

He looked so young, barely more than a boy, but he couldn't have been that much younger than Hestia herself.

"Come up to Exodus, Tia, so I can see you," the boy begged. "We can watch the sun rise over the Earth from space! You'll love it."

Vulcan waved his hand in the air, shaping light into the form now burned into his retinas. The boy Hestia had loved and lost. A jealous man might have hated him, but Vulcan felt nothing but sadness when he looked at the illusion. This boy had been lost like all the Academy dancers.

Hestia gasped, staring at the illusion

like it was a ghost.

"He's not real," Vulcan said, but she didn't seem to hear him.

She stalked up to the boy. "I should never have listened to you. I should have stayed on Earth, and waited for you, like I wanted. I never wanted to go into space, never wanted to leave Earth, but I loved you so much, I gave in, like I always did. But when you left the apartment, I closed all the window shades and tried to pretend I was studying at home, in my room. I got a job offer on Earth – a good one, in a library and everything. What I wanted. I was booked to take the space elevator down the day after New Year, but I couldn't find a way to tell you. And then you died, and I woke up here! Supernova swallow you, Ayumu, wherever you are, for stealing Earth and my family from me."

She turned her back and walked away.

Vulcan's hand trembled and the illusion wavered and died. That…was not what he'd expected.

"He's gone," he said softly, hoping she heard him.

Hestia gave a huge sniffle and swiped at her eyes. "Yes, and so is Earth. I'd been bottling that up for months, and I knew I'd have to tell him, but every time I tried…and then he died! Oh, how I hated him, for saving my life when all I'd wanted was to go home, and there was nothing I could do about it." She looked at him fiercely. "Now you know my deepest, darkest secret. I'm a horrible person. Maybe you should go back to your bar and leave me to drown my misery in a book. I'm poor company on the best of nights, and after that…" She shook her head. "What you must think of me. I did love him, I did, and I wanted to marry him, but I hated being in space so much, and every time I tried to tell him, he wouldn't listen!" She burst into tears.

Vulcan was no stranger to weeping women, though it had been a while since he'd comforted one. He wrapped her up in a hug, letting her cry into his shirt.

Slowly, her sobs subsided, and she looked up, swiping a hand across her face. "What you must think of me. I'm such a mess."

Vulcan looked down. "No more than

me." He ripped off the soaked shirt. "Better?"

She was staring again. "How did you do that?"

Stars, he'd done it without thinking. Well, she'd bared her soul to him. He could at least return the favour. "I have a dark secret, too. My audition for the Academy wasn't exactly conventional. It was a striptease in one of the private rooms of a sleazy strip club in the back alleys of Alba."

Nope, she hadn't stopped staring. "You slept your way to the top? I didn't think it was possible to do that any more!"

Vulcan laughed. "It would have taken some seriously supernatural sex to do that, and not even I'm that good. No, it was a striptease. A private show. I danced my bare arse off, but I definitely danced. I wouldn't have lasted a week in the Academy if I hadn't been good. None of the other dancers knew about my past. Just the instructor who paid for the private show."

Her mouth had dropped open. Stars, but she had a sweet mouth. Vulcan very much wanted to kiss her again, but now she knew he'd been a stripper, he doubted he'd get the chance.

"I don't believe you," Hestia said.

Vulcan looked around. The glass walls and ancient bookcases here in the Crypt were not the best place for a demonstration, but he found he very much wanted to give her one. "The grave's a fine and private place, but none,

I think, do there embrace. Take me somewhere you won't mind me bumping against the furniture, and I'll show you," he said.

Hestia pointed. "That way, to the stacks."

Through the glass-walled Crypt and through a set of sliding doors into a more mundane library, shelves full of ordinary books he could reach out and touch, plus a few scattered chairs. And a ladder…

Vulcan grinned. "This will do nicely."

THIRTEEN

Vulcan dragged one of the chairs into the middle of the room, then patted the seat. "If I'm to give you a private show, then you should have the best seat in the house."

Hestia obediently took her seat.

Vulcan looked around. "Now, all we need is some music. Something with a strong, fast beat…"

Hestia cleared her throat. "Computer, play a song suitable for Vulcan to dance to." At his look of surprise, she smiled. "This is a library. Its primary purpose is access to information. A voice activated search engine, as intuitive as the best on Earth, is essential."

"Madam Librarian, I have identified 32,689 suitable songs that match Vulcan's preferred dance style and past preferences. Ranked in order of best fit, would you like to hear a sample of the first search record?"

"Play it, computer," she said.

A solid drumbeat began, regular as a heartbeat, before the melody began to weave its way between the beats.

Vulcan's mouth dropped open. "That's

perfect," he said. "Can you get it to play the whole song?"

"Play the whole song from the beginning, computer."

"Of course, Madam Librarian."

The beat began again, but this time Vulcan moved with it.

Hestia's mind went blank.

FOURTEEN

Vulcan shook his head. The computer couldn't possibly have known this was the song he'd danced to in that long ago private audition back on Alba. Then, he'd been nervous, doing his first private show. But here in this secret library, with Hestia's eyes fixed on him, his mind filled with calm as the rest of his body bubbled with energy. The beat drummed through his bones, the melody coursing through his blood…it was like flying.

No, he was flying – dashing up the shelves like they were stairs, then somersaulting from the top of the bookcase to land in the centre of his impromptu stage. When the melody climbed again, so did he, jumping up to touch the ceiling before landing beside the ladder. Picking up the ladder in his arms, wishing he was holding her instead, he danced it to centre stage, right in front of Hestia.

He may have gotten a little carried away then, because he forgot that the bar uniform pants were made of stronger stuff than the ones Prochoros had provided for his dancers in Sin, with firmly stitched seams that did not tear apart at the slightest tug. After a few fruitless tries, he shrugged and decided it was better to dance with his pants on, anyway, especially as he wasn't wearing stage underwear underneath them.

As the last strains of the song died away, Vulcan held up his hands. "Normally, I'd take my clothes off as part of the performance, but I left all my costumes back on Alba. If you give me some time, I might be able to source something suitable here in the Colony, and then I could offer you a repeat performance. A better one."

Hestia shook her head. "That was amazing. I didn't know where to look as it was. That was…a lot sexier than your shows at Forge. I've never seen anything like it — not on Earth, or since." She fanned herself. "How can you…make me feel so much, just by watching you dance?"

Prochoros had said it was a gift, but Vulcan had heard the other dancers, both male and female, talk about private shows as foreplay, a prelude to more personal services that some of them provided. Sex clients paid a premium for. The key was getting the client so intent on the show that they wanted to be part of it.

Vulcan had never wanted to be that close to a member of the audience. Until now.

He held out his hand. "Come dance with me, and I'll show you," he offered.

Her eyes widened. "I can't dance the

way you do. My body doesn't flex like…"
She blushed.

Evidently she'd never been to a strip club on ladies' night before, where women – and some men – lined up to be allowed to join the dancers on stage.

"You won't have to. I'll do all the work," he coaxed.

Reluctantly, she rose and let him pull her into the middle of the room, every step stiff and resistant.

Then a new song started, and Vulcan knew he'd have to do things differently, or he'd lose her. And he didn't want to let her go.

He scooped her up in his arms, whirling her around as she clung to him. Slowly, she loosened her grip, as if realising that he wouldn't let her fall.

Then he caught sight of the ladder, and had a better idea. He lifted her onto one of the middle rungs, refusing to let his hands linger on her cute butt for any more than absolutely necessary, no matter how much he wanted to, and pinned her in place with his gaze alone. Now she was his fixed pole star, around which his whole world rotated, and every shift of his body was solely for her pleasure.

Before he'd realised it, the song was over, and the only sound was her panting breaths before she screamed, "Oh, oh….VULCAN!"

FIFTEEN

When the stars in her vision faded, Hestia found herself seated halfway up a stepladder, her skirt rucked up to her waist, with her legs wrapped firmly around Vulcan's hips, rubbing against him like some sort of animal in heat. Except that somehow, he'd managed to give her the most exquisite orgasm she'd ever experienced, and they still had their clothes on.

He leaned forward and touched his lips lightly to hers. "Right now, you are the most beautiful, desirable creature in the universe, and I have but one desire — to take you to bed right now, and worship your body as you deserve until dawn. But tell me you don't want the same thing, and I'll go home to a cold shower. Even if it takes half the underground reservoir to cool the burning desires you inspire. Tell me what you want from me, Hestia, and I'll give it to you. Anything you ask."

"You." The word came out hoarse and breathless. "I want…you. No one's ever made me feel like that before and I'm…burning for you a bit, too." She blushed, conscious of her soaked underwear between them.

"To the elevator, then," he said, lifting her off the ladder.

Only…she couldn't seem to unfasten her legs. She just wanted to stay wrapped around him forever, feeling the heat of him against her…

Her back hit something cool – the wall of the elevator – as her butt rested on the handrail that ran around the edges. She heard the rip of fabric, before air touched bare skin.

He held up her underwear, looking sheepish. "I'll buy you new ones."

She never wanted to wear underwear around him again. Not if it got between them…

Then his fingers were rubbing her,

slipping inside, and she could think of nothing else. Until she cried out, and cried out again. Three times. Three times she'd climaxed at his hands — each more mind-blowing than anything she'd experienced with Ayumu. And Vulcan hadn't even taken his pants off yet…

Somehow, they made it to her apartment, but her thoughts were hazy as to how. All she could think about was him, and the hard bulge between her thighs, and how much she hated his pants…

She couldn't say so, though, for mouth was too occupied with kissing him. She hadn't known tongues could dance like that, and she was breathless trying to keep up.

Her butt touched something cold —

he'd set her down on the shelf in her empty bookcase. She'd been meaning to get more shelves when she got more books, but right now, this was perfect. Hestia struggled to tug her dress over her head, before making short work of her bra. Her shoes were…somewhere…over there.

He had his hands on his pants, ready to unfasten them. "Stars, you're beautiful. More beautiful than I deserve," he breathed. "Are you sure you want to do this, Hestia?"

She laughed, and it came out as a high-pitched giggle. She felt lightheaded, from those three orgasms in quick succession. "If you don't take those pants off right now, I know I want to tear them off you. I'm the one who doesn't deserve you.

I'm…me…and you're built like a god."

"I'm just a man, but you…you're my goddess of inspiration. I want to worship you forever." Down came the pants, and that tempting bulge sprang free. "I should take you to the bed…"

Hestia couldn't wait any longer. "No. Here, now. Before I wake up from this dream."

He stalked toward her, all predator, yet she felt no fear. Only anticipation.

She swallowed. "They gave me a contraceptive implant when I woke from stasis, and a clean bill of health. Are you…?"

"Same — on both counts. I haven't been with a woman since before I left Alba. I haven't wanted anyone else since the moment I saw you."

This god wanted her? Tears sprang to her eyes. "Please," she begged.

She cried out as he entered her, entranced by how well they fit together.

"Perfect," he breathed, lifting her legs up onto his shoulders.

"What are you – oh!"

Reality retreated, and there was nothing else in the universe but two bodies twined into one in a dance as old and as hot as the sun.

Yet when she felt her pleasure about to peak, lights erupted around them, a thousand stars going nova all at once, before she joined them. She was only dimly aware of Vulcan stilling inside her, moaning her name.

When she opened her eyes, she found him smiling sheepishly at her. Her orgasm had faded to a soft, warm glow, but the light show hadn't abated.

"I hope you don't mind the fireworks. I was…that was…well, that's what you do to me," he said.

Hestia swallowed. Stars, but her throat was hoarse. She must have screamed louder than she'd realised. "So, you…liked it?" The best thing Ayumu had said about her lovemaking was that it wasn't bad, if he hadn't just shrugged and gone to sleep afterward. Fireworks were good, right?

Vulcan wrapped his arms around her and kissed her. "If every orgasm you give me is that good, I'm never going to want to get out of bed. And I've never lost control of my illusions like that before. I can't wait to do it again. But only if you do."

She laughed softly. "Of course I want to do that again. Happy New Year fireworks every night in bed with the star of the show? Now I know I'm dreaming."

"Then let's go to bed, so we can dream together," he said, holding out his hand.

Her legs still didn't want to let go of him. "You might have to carry me."

The words had scarcely left her lips before his arms were around her, under her, lifting her off the bookcase, pressing her body against his, on the way to her bed.

With all his dancer's stamina, it wasn't long before Vulcan was ready for her once more, intent on giving and receiving even more pleasure than their rushed first time. When fireworks burst above their heads for the second time, Hestia found herself shouting, "Happy New Year!"

"Happy New Year, my goddess, my inspiration," Vulcan replied, pressing a kiss to her breast, right over her heart. "May we spend many more together, for no New Year will be happy without you."

Or you, she thought lazily, stroking the muscles along his back.

When the first day of the New Year dawned, the light touched two bodies so intertwined, neither Hestia nor Vulcan could be sure where one of them ended and the other began. Hestia only hoped she started every New Year as happy as this.

SIXTEEN

Vulcan woke to Hestia sliding out of his arms. He reached for her, but somehow she'd already managed to get to the other side of the room. He sat up, blinking. How was it daylight already?

"I'm sorry, I need to go open the library," she said, genuine regret in her eyes. "You can stay and sleep if you want. I usually come home for lunch, and I can wake you then, if you like."

Tempting though the offer was, he should head home. He'd sleep better there, and he also wouldn't be tempted to sneak downstairs and drag Hestia down into the Crypt, for a repeat performance of last night. Stars, last night had been the best night of his life. His New Year was already off to a stellar start.

"I have end of year financials to do for Forge," he said. "But I would like to see you again. Any idea when that will be?"

She laughed softly. "Well, next New Year's Eve, at Forge, of course. I can't wait to see your next performance. If it's anything like the one you did downstairs, you'll need to turn up the cooling systems…or order in more drinks."

Vulcan shook his head. "There won't be a next performance. I'm done with mourning — time to move on. I…" He didn't know what he intended to do next. Just that he wanted his future to include her.

"You can't stop dancing. You're incredible at it. Your Academy or whatever might be gone, but you're the one with the talent, and you're still here. Still capable of delivering a mesmerising performance like no other. You are Forge."

He closed his eyes. "You don't understand."

"Blithering black holes I don't understand! I lost everything! My planet, my family, my job, the life I'd planned, the man I loved, and all the signed books I'd collected over the years. I haven't given up, no matter how many times I wanted to, and I won't let you give up either, Vulcan! You're the only bright spark in this city and I won't let you go out like that. If you won't get up on stage at Forge next New Year's Eve, I'll…I'll carry you up there myself!"

Vulcan laughed. She looked determined enough to do it, but there was no way she had the strength to actually manage such a feat.

"I can't," he said. "Every time I stepped onto that stage, it was a celebration of their lives. Though I might be the least of them, in honouring their spirits I could do it. Now…like I said, my mourning is over. The next time I step on stage, I'll be alone, and I don't have the kind of stage presence, the kind of experience, to hold the audience with a solo performance. And without the years of training I would have received at the Academy, I never will."

Hestia looked thoughtful. "Then…do something different. Maybe not at Forge, and not even New Year's Eve. What about the Thanksgiving Festival, to celebrate the Colony's one year anniversary? I know they're looking for entertainment. It's a celebration of a different sort. I know the organiser's boss. Actually, he has an overdue book at the moment. I could offer to waive his late fees if he brings the book in this week and finds a spot for you in the program…"

"But I've never performed alone."

She stamped her foot. "Of course you have – every time I've seen you dance, it's been just you and your illusions, though I didn't know they were illusions. Create a whole dance company, play them like puppets – it's your performance! Just do it. No more mourning, but a celebration of a year in the Colony."

"Only if you'll be there with me," he said.

"Me…on stage?" she squeaked.

He reached for her hands. "If you want, but you don't have to be. As long as you're there, all I have to do is look into your eyes, and it's like…almost as if I can feel that dream again, the dream I can dance."

She considered for a moment, then said, "All right. I'll be your date to the Thanksgiving Festival. You'll put on a performance then, and then we can discuss you dancing in the New Year at Forge."

Her mulish expression told him she wouldn't take no for an answer.

"Deal," he said.

He had no idea how he was going to accomplish what she'd asked for – stars, the festival organiser might turn him down flat, not wanting an ex-stripper on her entertainment schedule – but for Hestia, he was willing to try.

SEVENTEEN

Despite Hestia's protests, Reina had taken her shopping for a suitable dress to wear on her date with Vulcan. More clothing shops had appeared in the year since she'd last bought a dress – enough to make her consider wearing something other than the standard issue coveralls for everyday, instead of just special occasions. Like she had on Earth, before she'd lost her identity in the shapeless coveralls Exodus had provided for all its denizens, employee and dependent alike.

Today, her attention had been caught by a shop that had a display of brightly coloured scarves in the window. Something about the delicate swirls of colour had reminded her of Vulcan's light show. Perhaps if she wore one of those scarves with the dress she usually wore to Forge, Reina would agree to end the shopping expedition.

Until Hestia stepped inside the shop and saw that scarves were just the beginning.

A holographic mannequin walked around the shop, her outfit changing every few seconds. Dresses, suits, swimwear, lingerie…all in shimmering rainbow colours.

"Can I help you?"

Hestia blinked. The woman who'd spoken could have been the mannequin's twin, yet the dress she wore was white…at first. The more she looked, the more colours she saw, in pale pastel shades so subtle it was hard to be certain if they were really there, or a trick of shadows and light.

Tinkling laughter ran out, as the woman spread her skirts and did a little twirl. "You like it? I call this design Fading Dream, though I was tempted to call it Forgotten Memory. It's like grasping mist with your eyes." She looked appraisingly at Hestia. "I think the style would suit you, but the colour is too pale. Something brighter would bring out your eyes better. Come see the range, and we can work out the perfect combination for you."

At the shop counter, the woman pointed to the scarves spread out across the wall, stretching from the floor to the ceiling. Each a different design, some abstract, and some so realistic Hestia thought she could reach out and pluck the leaves from a particular scene.

"We take the design you choose, and print it on the style of clothing you wish. Rainbow Fish on your swimsuit, Parrot Playground on your playsuit, or Stellar Storm on your cocktail dress." As she said each option, the holographic model's outfit changed to match.

"Do you have anything like

fireworks?" Hestia asked, hardly daring to hope.

The woman smiled. "I call it Supernova. It really pops on shinier fabrics, especially silks and satins. I did some satin boxer shorts for a guy last week and…well, let's just say I'm jealous of his girlfriend."

For a moment, Hestia's mind flashed an image of Vulcan in his underwear, as well as out of it. "Can you put it on a dress…and maybe some matching lingerie to go underneath?" she asked.

Reina's jaw dropped. "You're going to sleep with the guy on the first date? You?"

Hestia turned bright red. She hadn't been able to bring herself to confess that Vulcan had stayed the night with her before they'd even been on a date, and now she didn't dare.

The woman at the counter grinned. "Lovely lingerie is never about the man, it's all about the woman wearing it. Sometimes it takes a dozen dates, and sometimes you know what you want in a matter of seconds. Love at first sight is real, though rare." She swiped at her tablet, then pushed it across the counter to Hestia. "What sort of dress are you after? Short and sexy, something more formal…?"

"It's for the Thanksgiving Festival," Hestia said.

The woman nodded. "So…something that goes from day into night, but is still good for dancing. Would you prefer a slit skirt, or something with a bit of twirl to it?" A few options flashed across the screen.

Hestia pointed at the one that showed the least flesh.

The woman nodded in approval. "Ah, the pinup dress. Yes, that's perfect for a Festival date."

Wait, pinup? Like naked centrefold sort of pinup? Hestia opened her mouth to tell the woman she'd changed her mind, but she'd already flitted across the shop, picking out a dress in shiny white, before slipping it over a dressmaker's dummy to have it printed.

"You're going to love this," the woman said.

Hestia closed her mouth, knowing it would be pointless to argue.

EIGHTEEN

Vulcan busied himself behind the bar while he waited for Hestia to arrive at Forge. He'd offered to pick her up, but she'd said she'd walk over, after closing the library for the day. Perhaps she wanted to see some of the entertainment on offer — there were certainly enough stages along the way. He'd been offered his pick of places and times for his performance – Rana, the organiser, had turned out to be a one of the Academy's season ticket holders, who'd never missed a show, and she'd admitted to almost hugging her boss when he'd told her Vulcan was interested in providing entertainment for the Festival. Funny, she hadn't even asked what the show would entail – just what he'd need, and when.

At first, he'd thought of using the stage in Forge, like he always did, but he wanted something that would really impress Hestia. His first idea had been a show of fireworks under the main Metropolis City dome, so he'd asked Rana for the ceiling of the dome as his stage, when night had fallen fully on the

Colony. She'd agreed, and he'd breathed a sigh of relief.

But as the day had progressed, watching the setup outside and seeing the sheer scale of the event, knowing everyone in the Colony would be out there watching, a bigger audience than he'd ever expected even at the Academy, he'd begun to think on a far grander scale. He performed for Hestia, an audience of one, but if the rest of the city liked his work, then maybe he should continue. Sure, he wasn't as talented as some of the stars of the Academy, but until someone with the talent and the training and the presence to take that role emerged, perhaps he might keep the crowd amused like a kind of cover band.

Tonight would tell.

"He's at the bar," Vulcan heard Anzo, the bouncer at the door, say.

Vulcan looked up, and beheld a vision.

It wasn't just him — every head in Forge turned to follow her progress. Hestia wore a shiny dress that caught the light, with a pattern of stars bursting into life. Or fireworks, like the ones suddenly surrounding her, lighting her up so that no one could possibly miss her.

That's when her eyes met his, and he could see her blush from across the room. "Vulcan! Are you doing that?" she asked, suddenly aware of all the eyes on her.

Stars, he was — that's what she did to him.

It was his turn to blush. "Ah, sorry. You just look so beautiful…"

Nihal made a retching sound. "Out, before you put the rest of our customers off their drinks. Or you make the staff sick, so then you'll have to serve behind the bar tonight. Go on your date, and enjoy the Festival."

Vulcan offered Hestia his arm. "Now let us sport while we may," he said.

She laughed. "Marvell, yes? You quoted him at New Year, too. Had we but world enough and time..."

Vulcan nodded. "But at my back I always hear time's winged chariot hurrying near." He paused, suddenly unsure. "Now, I guess this part's up to you. The Festival dinner is going to be served out in the square, a long table dinner for the whole city. If you want to be part of the crowd, and enjoy the

Festival that way, then we can order our drinks here and they'll bring them out to whichever table we choose. Or, if you prefer to enjoy the festivities a little apart from everyone else, I've prepared a place where you'll have the perfect view of my performance, as well as the rest of the city. Kind of like your library tower apartment, only a little more open to the night air."

"Or my balcony overlooking your stage. It's getting pretty crowded out there already. If I can still see the show without having to go out there where all the people are…" Hestia managed a watery smile. "I'd like that."

"Then tonight I shall show you the secrets behind the Forge!" Vulcan said, opening the STAFF ONLY door with a flourish. "Behold, the freight elevator!"

Instead of heading for the cellar, like he usually did, he pressed the button for the roof.

NINETEEN

When the elevator doors opened, Hestia stepped out onto the roof of the building. Above her, the night-dimmed lights reflected on the dome above, and below, she could see the whole city. All the people, the tables, the lights, the stages…it was the whole Colony, as she'd never seen it before.

And Vulcan…he'd understood her need to be apart from it all.

"Your private balcony table," Vulcan said, gesturing.

Hestia dragged her gaze from the view, and found him standing beside a small table for two, a table that looked exactly like the one they'd shared last New Year's Eve. Tonight, it was set for dinner, with a wine bottle already sitting in the ice bucket.

"Another bottle of priceless Earth wine? Vulcan, you can't!" she exclaimed.

Vulcan shrugged. "We don't have to open it if you don't want, but this is a special occasion. Besides, Forge's cellars are full of the stuff — there'll be a real Colony vintage sparkling before we're even halfway through the Earth stock.

Some of the rich bastards who expected to come here brought centuries' worth of precious books, while others brought a century's worth of wine."

"If you're sure," she said. She'd handled those precious books, for the sheer pleasure of it, so she could understand why Vulcan would want to drink the wine, as the vintner had intended.

"Here's Siofra with our dinner," Vulcan said, holding out a chair for Hestia.

She sat down, and was glad she had, for a winged woman appeared out of nowhere, carrying two covered plates.

"Thanks, Siofra. I'll let you know when we're ready for dessert," Vulcan said.

The woman nodded, then flew over

the edge of the roof.

Hestia waited until she was sure the girl was out of earshot. "Were those wings real?" she whispered.

Vulcan laughed. "You need to get out more. Siofra's a sprite, and there are quite a few of them here in the Colony. None can cook as well as Siofra, though, which is why we have an understanding. Forge provides her with the best ingredients, and she agrees to work for me, creating whatever she wishes for the menu. She turned her nose up at the standard issue vat beef for the Festival, so if you want a steak, I'll have to get Nihal to order one in from one of the neighbours' kitchens, but whatever this is, I'm sure it's the best food available in the Colony tonight."

Hestia swallowed. "I haven't eaten anything but ration bars since I left Earth. They were standard issue for employees and their families on Exodus, and we couldn't afford to waste money on luxuries. Here, they were in the kitchen at my house, and I've never been much of a cook, so…I'm sure it'll be the best meal I've eaten in years." She lifted the cover and inhaled deeply. Oh, if heaven existed, that's what it smelled like. She picked up her cutlery and took a bite. Stars, it tasted even better.

This was living. So much better than just surviving.

"Wow, I don't think I've ever seen anyone eat so fast," Vulcan said.

Hestia looked down. How could her dinner be gone?

"I can comm down to the kitchen for another serve, or would you like me to ask Siofra to bring up dessert?"

The thought of eating any more right now was more than Hestia could take. "I truly think I've had enough. It was just so good."

Vulcan laughed softly. "You definitely need to get out more. How about dinner tomorrow? Or the day after?" He ducked his head. "Actually, I'm hoping you'll say both. The sooner we get you off those horrible ration bars, the better. I consider it my civic duty."

Now it was Hestia's turn to laugh. "They're not that bad, once you get used to them. Nutritionally balanced, no cooking required…and there were plenty of them aboard the Genesis. Enough to sustain everyone aboard for a decade."

Vulcan shuddered. "I guarantee you wouldn't have been the only suicidal passenger during the first year, if it had come to that. Shipwreck survivors in the pre-space centuries on Earth showed us that — despair is a far more effective killer than starvation. There's more to life than simple survival. People need hope, no matter how small."

Hestia nodded. "Panem and circenses, or bread and games. Juvenal, I think. I had books — all the entertainment I need."

"Ah, but you came to Forge, too — and that's why you're here, isn't it? Because I promised to perform." Vulcan set down his cutlery on his now empty plate. "And here comes time's winged chariot, right on cue. Come." He rose and held out his hand.

Hestia took it, and let him lead her to a sofa near the edge of the roof, where she had an uninterrupted view across Metropolis City. Vulcan sat next to her.

"Ready?" he asked.

At her nod, he grinned. Then all the lights went out, all across the city.

Gasps and screams came from the streets below.

Then two glowing clouds appeared, on opposite sides of the city. One had streaks of light darting through it, like red lightning or laser fire. The other glowed orange in the centre, as if something had exploded or caught fire.

Out of the red streaked cloud stepped a robot, firing wildly with a laser weapon, before it vanished into the cloud again.

The orange cloud dispersed, revealing the space station that had been Exodus shipyard, one end still belching smoke from the fire that had claimed Ayumu's life.

Both images spun, faster and faster, until a figure emerged from each cloud of smoke, which boarded a ramp like the ones Hestia had seen on the Genesis before doors slid shut and hid the figures from sight.

The images spun again, morphing from clouds into ships. One Hestia recognised as the Genesis, so she imagined the other, similar craft had to be the Titanic, the lost Titan colony ship.

The ships stood still, as a galaxy of stars materialised around them. Then the ships began to dance, first at opposite sides of the dome, before passing closer and closer to each other, until they met before a glowing red star: Altan.

Now the dance quickened, becoming a chase through asteroids and planets, as they whirled around that central red star. Laser fire streaked across the dome, or at least that's what it looked like, as beams of light spat out of each of the phantom ships.

Then two silver streaks shot out of the ships, and it was their turn to dance. It took Hestia a moment to realise they were shuttles, weaving through the system until they approached a second red sphere: the planet of New Hope, with the Colony little more than a silver blister upon its rocky surface. But the planet grew and grew, until a misty red landscape spread across the dome above.

The shuttles landed, so close together the might be kissing, and a figure emerged from each of them. The two figures joined hands, then disappeared into the silver dome of the Colony.

The image spun, red mist fading to silver, showing glimpses of Metropolis City and the interior of each of the domes. Trees, water, fields, the Arena…before two figures formed on opposite sides of the cloud. Two people who looked very much like Vulcan and Hestia.

They danced, never quite touching, between trees and buildings and aircars, before the background became the open square in front of Forge.

With no obstacles between them any more, the couple linked hands, then kissed. The moment their lips touched, the whole image exploded into fireworks. When the fireworks faded, the words HAPPY ANNIVERSARY COLONISTS appeared in the sky, before a new set of fireworks exploded around them.

Vulcan waited a few seconds for the words to disperse, before waving his hand. All the lights came back on.

Below, the cheering started, louder than anything Hestia had heard at Forge, when Vulcan had performed on stage.

This was the sound of a whole city screaming their approval for a masterful performance.

High above the city, two figures

appeared again. Both bowed to the crowd, and the applause was drowned out by the drumming of feet on the paving. Vulcan had earned himself a standing ovation for his solo performance.

Hestia grinned. "You have to perform on New Year's Eve now, or I think there'll be a riot."

Vulcan turned to her. "Tonight's performance was for an audience of one. Did you like it?"

"I loved it. Though I was hoping you'd take centre stage, instead of just your illusions." She wet her lips. "Actually, the more important question is what did you think of it? This is your art, your talent, on display. This isn't like any of your earlier performances I've seen. Is this your plan for the future?"

Vulcan laughed. "This was a fun experiment, to see how grand I could make my illusions, and what people would say. What you would say. I never plan a performance, it just sort of…happens…when I first hear the music, and I refine it from there. The only plans I'd like to make for the future are ones that involve you."

Hestia stretched. "Do they also involve this sofa, or somewhere more private?"

"We can go down to my apartment, if you like. Just like you, I live above where I work. You're very welcome to stay."

Hestia half expected to hear Sunita's voice telling her to live a little, but her head was mercifully silent. Instead, she looked up at Vulcan. "If I stay, I'll expect another performance like New Year's Eve," she said.

Vulcan took her hands, just like the illusions had done in the sky above. "For you, anything."

Then he kissed her, and she forgot everything else, until shouts rose up from the street below.

Hestia looked up into a shower of fireworks, lighting up the dome above. She felt her face grow hot.

"See? You light up the night sky like it's day. There's probably poetry about that, somewhere, but I can't think of anything but you when you look at me like that," Vulcan said. He leaned forward and kissed her again.

More shouts from the street. Stars,

could they see them kissing?

"Take me to bed, and I promise next year's library theme will be poetry," Hestia said.

Vulcan scooped her up in his arms. "Your wish is my command."

TWENTY

Hestia smoothed her dress as she stepped into Forge. She'd worn her Festival dress this time, instead of the black one, because New Year was definitely a time for fireworks.

Nihal stood at the bar, acknowledging Hestia with a nod. "Your table is waiting, with a bottle of wine on ice, compliments of the house. Unless you'd like a cocktail first?"

Hestia shook her head. Tonight, she didn't want to forget. She wanted to watch, and remember.

She took her familiar seat on the balcony, thanking the waiter who poured her a glass of champagne. She barely had a moment to sip it before the lights went dark.

A deep, steady beat rose from the floor, vibrating through her feet as it filled the bar with the thumping sound, silencing all conversation.

Once again, Hestia found herself perched eagerly on the edge of her seat, awaiting the show. The drumming heartbeat quickened, until it beat as fast as her own thrumming heart.

And there he was, standing in the centre of the stage, staring right at her.

Hestia couldn't help but smile.

When he moved, he became her entire galaxy, like there was nothing and no one else in the universe. Just the two of them.

Of course, the crowd of illusions dancing around him in perfect synchrony made it look otherwise, but Hestia knew they were just satellites to his blazing sun.

"More wine, miss?"

Hestia tore her eyes away from the stage to find a grinning Vulcan standing beside her in his bar blacks, wine bottle in hand.

"How…?" she began, looking from him to the stage and back again.

The music stopped and the illusion dancers bowed in unison, before vanishing in a cloud of smoke, to tumultuous applause.

"Master of illusion, that's me," he said. "Besides, I'm saving myself for a private performance for you tonight. I was talking to Melete, who owns the Black Cat Cabaret, and she gave me the details of the designer who creates all their costumes. I think you'll like what we came up with, but the best place to show you is that Crypt of yours, in the room with the ladder…"

Hestia blinked, but the vision of Vulcan dancing shirtless in the Crypt wouldn't go away. She didn't want it to, either.

"I promise I'll seduce you so

thoroughly, it'll put Marvell and all the other poets to shame. Romance beyond your wildest dreams," Vulcan whispered.

Hestia didn't need Sunita's voice to urge her on tonight. She rose, tucking her arm into Vulcan's. "What are we waiting for? It sounds like you're planning the happiest New Year ever. And I want it all."

Tonight, old acquaintance would definitely be forgotten, if only for a little while. So much had changed in one short year. Out with the old, and in with the new. A Happy New Year indeed.

ABOUT THE AUTHOR

Demelza Carlton has always loved the ocean, but on her first snorkelling trip she found she was afraid of fish.

She has since swum with sea lions, sharks and sea cucumbers and stood on spray drenched cliffs over a seething sea as a seven-metre cyclonic swell surged in, shattering a shipwreck below.

Demelza now lives in Perth, Western Australia, the shark attack capital of the world.

The *Ocean's Gift* series was her first foray into fiction, followed by her suspense thriller *Nightmares* trilogy. She swears the *Mel Goes to Hell* series ambushed her on a crowded train and wouldn't leave her alone.

Want to know more? You can follow Demelza on Facebook, Twitter, YouTube or her website, Demelza Carlton's Place at:

www.demelzacarlton.com

More Books by Demelza Carlton

Colony: Aqua series

Halcyon (#1)

Poseidon (#2)

Apollo (#3)

<u>**Siren of Secrets series**</u>

Ocean's Secret (#1)

Ocean's Gift (#2)

Ocean's Infiltrator (#3)

<u>**Nightmares Trilogy**</u>

Nightmares of Caitlin Lockyer (#1)

Necessary Evil of Nathan Miller (#2)

Afterlife of Alana Miller (#3)

<u>**Mel Goes to Hell series**</u>

The Devil's Work (#1)

See You in Hell (#2)

Mel Goes to Hell (#3)

To Hell and Back (#4)

The Holiday From Hell (#5)

All Hell Breaks Loose (#6)

The Devil Goes to Heaven (#7)

<u>**Romance Island Resort series**</u>

Maid for the Rock Star (#1)

The Rock Star's Email Order Bride (#2)

The Rock Star's Virginity (#3)

The Rock Star and the Billionaire (#4)

The Rock Star Wants A Wife (#5)

The Rock Star's Wedding (#6)

Maid for the South Pole (#7)

Romance a Medieval Fairytale series

Enchant: Beauty and the Beast Retold

Dance: Cinderella Retold

Fly: Goose Girl Retold

Revel: Twelve Dancing Princesses Retold

Silence: Little Mermaid Retold

Awaken: Sleeping Beauty Retold

Embellish: Brave Little Tailor Retold

Appease: Princess and the Pea Retold

Blow: Three Little Pigs Retold

Return: Hansel and Gretel Retold

Wish: Aladdin Retold

Melt: Snow Queen Retold

Spin: Rumpelstiltskin Retold

Kiss: Frog Prince Retold

Reflect: Snow White Retold

Roar: Goldilocks Retold

Cobble: Elves and the Shoemaker Retold

Float: Enchanted Horse Retold

Steal: Forty Thieves Retold

Call: Pied Piper Retold

Fall: Scheherazade Retold

Feather: Swan Maidens Retold

Cross: Billy Goats Gruff Retold

Weave: Rapunzel Retold

Claim: Puss in Boots Retold

Curse: Rose Red Retold